The Mythology and Traditions of the Dieguenos

By

Constance Goddard Du Bois

First published in 1901

Published by Left of Brain Books

Copyright © 2023 Left of Brain Books

ISBN 978-1-397-66990-2

First Edition

PUBLISHER'S PREFACE

About the Book

"Kumeyaay traditional narratives include myths, legends, tales, and oral histories preserved by the Kumeyaay (Ipai, Tipai, Kamia, Diegueno) people of southern California and northwestern Baja California.

Kumeyaay oral literature is very similar to that of their Yuman relatives to the south and east, as well as to that of their Uto-Aztecan neighbors to the north. Particularly prominent are versions of the Southern California Creation Myth and of the long Flute Lure myth."

(Quote from wikipedia.org)

CONTENTS

THE MYTHOLOGY OF THE DIEGUENOS

THE MYTHOLOGY OF THE DIEGUEÑOS

by Constance Goddard Du Bois

THE Diegueños have been classified as belonging to the Yuman family of Turner and Brinton. They make part of the Mission Indians of San Diego County, California, in which are also included fragments of Shoshonean tribes, akin to the Nahuatlan peoples of Southern Mexico. It would not be surprising to find in the folklore of the Shoshonean tribes traces of Aztec influence; but if the Diegueños belong to another family, a rather curious problem is presented by the following relics of tribal mythology related to me by old Cinon Duro, the last chief of the Diegueños, since they seem to suggest by internal evidence relations with primitive Aztec tradition.

THE STORY OF THE CREATION

WHEN Tu-chai-pai made the world, the earth is the woman, the sky is the man. The sky came down upon the earth. The world in the beginning was pure lake covered with tules. Tu-chai-pai and Yo-ko-mat-is, the brother, sat together, stooping far over, bowed down under the weight of the sky. The Maker said to the brother, "What am I going to do?"

"I do not know," said Yo-ko-mat-is.

"Let us go a little farther," said the Maker.

Then they went a little farther and sat down again. "Now, what am I going to do? " said Tu-chai-pai.

"I do not know."

All this time Tu-chai-pai knew what he would do, but he was asking the brother.

Then he said, "We-hicht, we-hicht, we-hicht," three times; and he took tobacco in his hand, and rubbed it fine, and blew upon it three times, and every time he blew the heavens rose higher above their heads. Then the boy did the very same thing, because the Maker told him to do it. The heavens went high, and there was the sky. Then they did it both together, "We-hicht, we-hicht, we-hicht;" and both took the tobacco, and rubbed it, and puffed upon it, and sent the sky up, so-- (into a concave arch).

Then they placed the North, South, East and West. Tu-chai-pai made a line upon the ground.

"Why do you make that line?"

"I am making the line from East to West, and I name them thus, Y-nak, East; A-uk, West. Now you may make it from North to South."

Then Yo-ko-mat-is was thinking very much.

"Why are you thinking?"

"Oh, I must think; but now I have arranged it. I draw a line thus (a crossline), and I name it Ya-wak, South; Ka-tulk, [1] North."

"Why have we done this?"

"I do not know."

"Then I will tell you. Three or four men are coming from the East, and from the West three or four Indians are coming."

The boy asked, "And do four men come from the North, and two or three men come also from the South?"

Then Tu-chai-pai said, "Now I am going to make hills and valleys, and little hollows of water."

"Why are you making all these things?

---

[1] Or Ka-tulch; it has a guttural sound.

The Maker said, "After a while, when men come and are walking back and forth in the world, they will need to drink water, or they will die." He had already put the ocean down in its bed, but he made these little waters for the people.

Then he made the forests, and said, "After a while men will die of cold unless I make wood for them to use. What are we going to do now?"

"I do not know."

"We are going to dig in the ground, and take mud, and make the Indians first." And he dug in the ground, and took mud, and made of it first the men, and after that the women. He made the men very well, but he did not make the women very well. It was much trouble to make them, and it took a longtime. He made a beard for the men and boys, but not for the women. After the Indians he made the Mexicans, and he finished all his making. Then he called out very loud, "You can never die, and you can never be tired, but you shall walk all the time." After that he made them so that they could sleep at night, and need not walk around all the time in the darkness. At last he told them that they must travel towards the East, towards the light.

The people walked in darkness till he made the light. Then they came out and searched for the light, and when they found it they were glad. Then be called out to make the moon, and he said to the other, "You may make the moon as I have made the sun. Some time it is going to die. When it grows very small, men may know that it is going to die, and at that time all men, young and old, must run races."

All the pueblos talked about the matter, and they understood that they must run these races, and that Tu-chai-pai was looking at them to see that they did this. After the Maker did all this he did nothing more, but he was thinking many days.

THE FLY AT THE COUNCIL

TU-chai-pai thought to himself, "If all my sons do not have enough food and drink, what will become of them?" After he thought of that a long time he said, "Then theywould die." Then he said, "What do my men want to do? I will give them three choices, to die now forever, or to live for a time and return, or to live forever."

When he had finished thinking, he called all the men together, but not the women; and he said to them, "I was thinking; there is not much food and water now. I want to know what you wish to do, and I will give you three choices; to die forever, to live for a time and return, or to live forever." Some of the people said, "We want to die now forever." Others said, "We want to live for a time and return." Others said, "We want to live forever." So they talked and they talked, and they did not know what to do.

Then the fly came and said, "Oh, you men, what are you talking so much about? Tell him you want to die forever." So they talked and they talked very much, and they made this choice, to die and to be done with life, and to die forever. This is the reason the fly rubs his hands together. He is begging forgiveness of the people for these words.

THE IMPIETY OF THE FROG

WHEN the moon had grown very little all the people were over there running races; and after all had finished running, the rabbit and the frog ran together; and all the people stood around looking on and laughing at the frog, because he had the shape of a man, but wore no clothes. Then the frog was very angry at the Maker, and the thought entered his head, "Because you did not make me well, you shall pay for it."

Tu-chai-pai had gone away to a very high place, and he was asleep up there, and the frog was down in a deep place holding up his hands in defiance of the Maker. Then came the sunshine, and Tu-chai-pai with it. He had a long stick, pointed at both ends, and he held it up over his head. And he took the stick and felt in the deep place with it, and it touched the back of the frog, where it made a long white mark. By that time the frog had planned a wrong deed. He meant to exude poison, swallow it, and die. When thoughts of this evil entered the heart of Tu-chai-pai, he said to himself, "I shall die." Then some boys came and told him what the frog had done.

Tu-chai-pai said, "I shall die with the moon. Go, look at the moon, Ach-hulch-la-tai. Look again, Hup-lach-sen. Look at it a third time, Hucht-la-kutl. [1] Then I will die."

"Oh, it is a bad time." They looked at the moon, and they watched it to see when Tu-chai-pai would die. It was very little,

---

[1] Are these the phases of the moon?

and they watched it grow smaller, and in six months he finished his life. And all the things on this earth are the children of Tu-chai-pai, and they will die, too.

THE FIESTA OF THE DEATH OF TU-CHAI-PAI

AS soon as they found that Tu-chai-pai was dead, all living things came together from the mountains and the valleys, all men and all animals to mourn for him. The dove that lives here went away to seek her mate upon a high white mountain, and when she came back there was blood on her wings, the blood of her father. Then they went on a high mountain, and set up two tablets, one to the East, and another to the West, and on these tablets were written the number of the days of the fiesta of the death of Tu-chai-pai.

So the men wanted to bury him, and they made a great funeral pyre, and were going to set fire to it, but the coyote would not agree to this, and the men were afraid of him. So the men sent him very far to the East; and when he was far away he saw the plume of smoke rising up, and came hurrying back.

"What are you burning?"

"We are burning nothing."

Then they sent him away again, far towards the sunset; but when he looked back again he saw the smoke. By that time the body was burned, all but the heart. And now the coyote came back.

So the men stood close together, shoulder to shoulder, about the heart of Tu-chai-pai. The coyote said, "I see what you are burning;" and he sprang over the heads of the men, seized the heart, fled to the mountain, and devoured it. For this reason men hate the coyote.

Then Yo-ko-mat-is, the brother, went far away to the West, but when men pray to him for rain, he comes back and answers their prayers.

Since the Mission Indians were long ago converted and civilized by the early Spanish friars, one is tempted at first to emphasize in this mythology certain resemblances to Christian teachings; but if the reader is sufficiently interested in the subject to give it further study, he will find that such resemblances are for the most part misleading. Let him consult, in this connection, Brinton's "Myths of the New World," pp. 67, 132, 171, 194, 226, and 255; and "American Hero Myths," by the same author, pp. 55, 75, 103, and 125. The latter references will convince him that the correlated ideas of the death of the Maker, the frog, the moon, the coyote, the funeral pyre, and the unconsumed heart are genuine fragments of Aztec folk-lore. To compare this story in its resemblances and differences with the folk-lore of the Indians of Northern California, he should refer to Powers's monograph in the "U. S. Geographical and Geological Survey of the Rocky Mountain Region," vol. iii.

Constance Goddard Du Bois.

A STORY OF THE CHAUP

THE STORY OF THE CHAUP: [1]

A MYTH OF THE DIEGUEÑOS [2]

THERE were once two young girls who were sisters, and at this time there was a house made of earth where the Young men used to sleep at night, and they talked about the girls who were sisters, and wanted to marry them, but they could not talk to them themselves, so they told the gopher to go speak to them, and this the gopher was very glad to do.

The girls used to go very early every morning to swim in a pool of water, and the gopher knew that the girls went there to swim, and one morning before it was light he went over there to the pool and got into the water and hid himself.

The sisters came down as usual to the water, but it did not look the same to them as on every other day. The girls sang

In-ya-há
Mi-ka-yá-ya
In-ya-há-ha
Mi-ka-yá, etc.

It was cloudy and troubled and they were afraid to enter it.

---

[1] Chaup is the name for shooting-star, or rather for the great fire-balls of electric or meteoric origin which are sometimes seen in the clear air of the Southwest, illuminating the ground with a bright light and accompanied by a sound like thunder. Chaup is the same as Taquish of the Cahuillas in some of his characteristics.
[2] Copyright, 1904, by CONSTANCE GODDARD Du BOIS.

Song: He-yám He-yó, etc.

But day was dawning and the elder said, "Jump in, my little sister. There is nothing to fear."

"Oh, no. It is you who must go first. It is never suitable for young people to do things in advance of their elders."

Song: He-hán-ha-wé
He-yám-he-hó, etc.

So the elder sister entered the pool; and though the gopher was close beside her in the water he did not speak to her; but when the younger sister plunged into the water he came near to her.

Screaming with terror, she ran from the water, and called out to her sister that something had been near her in the water, but she did not know what it was. She was suffering. So the elder sister built a great fire and put an olla full of water on to heat, and put some of the sage plant in the water, and the younger bathed with it and was well.

Song: O-cha-wha-tchi-sa
Hay-cha-wha-tchi-sa, etc.

After this the younger sister was going to have twin babies. (Song.) And she went to the water and sang about it that this was the place where she used to swim. (Song.) When she got out of the water she was so weak that she had to use a stick to help her steps, and when she went into her house she took one of the great -baskets and leaned against it singing sad songs and fearing she was going to die. (Song.) Already she had named her little twins. One she called Par-a-han, and the other A-shat-a-hutsch. (Song: Same as last.)

When the babies were born both of the sisters fell into a faint, and when the elder came to herself there was a little baby boy upon the ground, and she look it upon her lap rejoicing. (Song.) Again they both became unconscious, and again the elder sister, coming to herself, was glad to see a little baby boy upon the ground, and she took the two together upon her lap. (Song.)

(One of the earliest offices of care for the new-born infants required the use of a knife), and the sisters did not know what to do. They tried to use a piece of charcoal, until the elder sister, who was a witch-doctor and knew everything, stood tip and held her hand to the north and brought down a red stone; and when she got home she broke it (chipped it?) into a sort of a knife.

Then she held up her hands to the south and got a blue stone of the same sort. (Song.) And the mother used the knives for first one and then the other of the babies.

And the two sisters were so happy playing with the little twins that they could not stop to eat or sleep. They painted the babies' bodies with red paint, a sort of clay that is found beside the water. "They need a cradle [1] now," said the elder sister, "but they have no father to bring them what they need. They will never know a father's care."

But the two sisters went up upon the mountain and found little long sticks, and they bent them and made cradles out of them. They did not know how to do it, but they made them any way to hold the babies. (Song.)

They sang while they made them that they didn't know how, but they would do to hold the babies. (Song.)

---

[1] Baby basket

They finished the cradles and put the babies in them, and they wove coverings for their heads. (Song.)

Then the elder sister held up her hand to the north and got a basket, not a good one, for it was roughly made; and this she put upon the elder baby's head. Then she held up her hand to the south and got another basket. This time it was a fine one, and this she put upon the younger baby's head. (Song.) And the mother named the babies, but to both she gave the name Cuy-a-ho-marr.

All the people were playing ball one day, hitting the ball upon the ground with a stick; and the coyote was playing with them all day long; but when it drew towards sunset the coyote looked up and said: "It is time for me now to go home to my children and their mother, who are waiting for me in the house. [1] I must take some wood home with me."

So he went to a big fallen tree, chopped off an armful, and went to the house where the mother of the twins was sick in bed. She had a stick near her bed, and when she saw the coyote coming in on his lying errand she picked up the stick and chased him out of the house, so that he ran far away to the north. (Song.) She sang that since no one knew the father of the twins the coyote thought he could make sport of her.

After that a little wild canary, who had also been watching the game of ball, said: "It is time for me to go home to my family, who are waiting for me in the house." So, like the coyote, he went to the fallen tree, chopped an armful of wood, and went to the woman's house. "Where are you, my dear wife?" he called. The woman hurried to the door, but when she saw that

---

[1] Brush hut, translated "house" by educated Indian interpreter.

it was only a wild canary she grew very angry, and hit him with the stick and chased him out into the bushes.

Song: He-yo-ho-ree, etc.

You are only a silly bird," she sang. "The people that come after us will kill you and eat you at a mouthful."

One day the mother said to her sister, "Why don't you go and collect the seeds of the sage? They are withering and ready to fall. Why do you keep so close about the house? You have no children to tend. Go far away and work. As for me, I will gather those that grow near the house."

So she shut the little babies in the house, and for a door she rolled a big log from the south against the opening. And as she started to pick the seeds she heard the log talking: 'Oh yes, I will put the babies to sleep. They are my own little children."

So she hurried back into the house, nursed the babies, and put them to sleep herself.

The metate stone was weeping as she passed it. There is a sort of water that runs down, and they say the stone is weeping. It was upside down, and she sang a song,-- to tell it she had no time to grind on it, for her children kept her so busy with work for them.

In-ya-ha, etc.,--

The babies were growing fast, and the mother sang to them that they had no father. She did not know who or where he was.

Song: Mai-to-wak,
Me-awa-hum,
Ya-wa-ham,
Mi-ay-o-ham,
Hai-to-wak
So-lo-ham
Hai-to-wak
Mi-ay-o-ham, etc.

Meaning of the song: They had no father, no one to lead them by the hand. They would never know their father, and would die without knowing him.

One day the mother and her sister went away again to gather the sage seeds. The seed that they bad already brought home they had spread out on a great flat rock to dry. They left the little babies hanging in their cradles outside the house; and the quails came and began eating the seeds.

The babies in their cradles were talking together.

"Jump down, brother," said the younger baby, "and drive the quails away."

"Do it yourself."

"It would not be right for me to do that. The younger should wait for the older," was the answer.

With that they both jumped down, and went into the house, where they found a bow and arrow, and tried to shoot the quails. But they hit nothing, and the quails flew off a little way and then returned. The little babies sat on the ground and did not know what to do.

"What ails you, brother?" said the younger. You said that you knew all things. Why can't you kill the quails?"

With that the older brother began shaking his head, and great hailstones came out of his ears. The younger did the same, until the ground was piled with hailstones, and then they made a sling and with the hailstones shot and killed all the quail and left them lying on the ground. (Song.) All were killed but one, which they caught in their hands and held on their laps until they hurt it, and then they let it go. It was the quail who sang the song because of his joy in being free, but the brothers answered, "You are glad now, but you won't be glad in the future. The people who come after us will kill you in just the same way." (Song.)

The boys then made some ropes of twisted straw and played with them until sunset; but as it grew late they began to fear that their mother would find they had left their cradles, so they took all the dead quails and tied them to the rope and hung them about inside the house, until the house was full of them. Then they got into their cradles.

When the mother came home and saw the quails hung within the house she said, "I have a husband then, who fills my house with game," and full of anger she cut the rope and threw the quails away.

One of the babies began to cry and the sister went and took him down and brought him to the mother to nurse, but the baby refused to nurse and cried the more. Then the other cried and would not nurse, and the more the women tried to still them, the harder they both cried.

"What can ail them?" said the sisters. "Is it the red ants that are stinging them?" They took off all the babies' clothes to look for the red ants, but still the children cried.

"Perhaps they cry because I threw the quails away," said the mother. "It may have been they who killed them. Go build a fire and let us cook the birds."

So they built a great fire and cooked and ate the birds, and then the babies were content.

Song: Yá-ká-cha-wáh, etc.

Then the mother and her sister went away to another home, and took the babies with them; but the sister got lost on the way, and the mother was left alone.

One day she went away from home and left the babies hanging in their cradles; but thinking that they might come down from their cradles and do something on the sly, she determined to stay close at hand and watch what might happen. So she changed herself into the stump of a tree growing not far away.

As soon as she was out of sight the babies jumped down from their cradles, and made themselves little bows and arrows, with which they began playing in the house; then they ran out of doors to where the mother stood in the shape of a stump. The elder brother hurried past her without a glance, but the younger called out to him, "Be careful, brother, what you do. I see something strange."

"Come on," said the elder brother. "What are you afraid of?

"Come back, I say," repeated the younger. "There is surely something worth looking at here."

"What is it you mean?" asked the elder, running back.

"Look," said his brother, pointing at the stump.

"Oh, that is nothing but the stump of a tree, the sort that small boys use as a mark to shoot at."

"If that is so I'll hit it," said the younger, raising his bow.

"So will I," said the elder.

Just as they pointed their arrows at the stump the mother called out to them, "Wicked boys, is that the way you treat the mother who worked and cared for you when you were small and helpless? Just as soon as you grow large you wish to kill me. The people who come after us will tell the story of the bad boys who killed their mother."

Song: Ha-chaup
In-ya-ka-ha, etc.

With that she came to them in her own shape and patted them on the cheeks, for she saw that they were angry at her chiding; but they turned their heads away and would not listen to her. Instead of mother they called her Sin-yo-hauch [1]--the woman who had been turned into a stump.

But she caressed them until they were content again, and she promised to make them bows and arrows and teach them how to hunt.

---

[1] This is also the name of the Earth-Mother, very sacred to the older Indians. Those who have been under Spanish influence identify her with the Virgin Mary.

So she sent one to the north and the other to the south to get the right sort of wood to make arrows. In the evening they came back each with a great bundle of sticks. The mother was very glad when she saw it and said: "The people who come after us will make arrows as I am going to do."

So she went to where there was a big pile of ashes and cleaned the wood for the arrows, and put them on top of the house to dry in the sun. (Song.)

Next day she made the arrows from the wood for the little boys, but she made the arrows for the younger son the best.

And she told them to go to bed very early that night, so they could get up betimes in the morning and go to a hill very far away where a willow-tree grew, which they must cut down and bring home to her that out of it she might make them bows. They went as she told them and cut the willow-tree and brought it home, asking if that was the wood she meant.

"It is," she answered, and she split it in lengths and made two bows, one for the elder and one for the younger, but the bow of the younger was the better.

That night the boys could not sleep for wishing for the day when they might go hunting.

Song: In-ya-ke-te-me-
Hi-Ilya, etc.

As soon as it was light they hurried forth, and saw not far from their home a big lizard with a blue breast lying on a rock. They were so frightened that they hastened home. "What ails you?" asked the mother, and when they told her of the monster they had seen she told them that that was a thing to shoot for food; so they went and killed it and brought it home.

They went out again, and not so far away they saw a big rat building its house, and they ran home as fast as they could go.

"What ails you?" asked the mother anxiously. "Have you been bitten by a rattlesnake?"

"Oh, mother, we saw something building a house, and it had a great long tail." "Why, that is something that is good to eat." So they went out and killed it and brought it home.

Next time they went they saw a little rabbit, and, running home as fast as their legs would carry them, they told their mother that they had seen something gray walking about. "Why, that was nothing but a rabbit, and very good to eat." So they went and killed it and brought it home.

Next day they saw a big hare, and, half scared to death, they told their mother that something with great long ears was walking about. "It is a hare, my children, a thing that is good to eat." So they went out and shot it and brought it home.

Next day they went again and saw a big deer, and, more frightened than ever before, they ran home to their mother.

"Oh, mother, we have seen a thing that is walking about with a tree growing out of its had."

"Now that is a deer," said the mother, "a thing that you must not kill by yourselves, but you must call all the people together, and all go on the hunt and each have a share of the meat."

But the little boys would not listen to their mother, for they were determined to kill the deer by themselves. So the next day they went and chased and killed the deer, and left it lying while they went to tell their mother what they had done.

She would not believe that they had done this, for it was not the right way to do. Many must eat of that meat.

"Come, hurry, mother," said the boys; "bring knives and cut it open and let us carry it home." The mother did not want to go, but, urged by her sons, she followed them to where they had left the deer.

"I see, my sons, that you have disobeyed me and killed the deer, but we cannot carry it home. We must skin it here and cut it up, for that is the way to do. The people who come after us will do as we do, not carry a deer home, but skin it in the mountains where they kill it."

Song: Kwa-kwe-kwa-hm, etc.

"Bring grass to lay the pieces upon as I cut it," said the mother, and the boys began to gather the grass near at hand.

"No, that grass is not good," said the mother. "Go farther off and bring a heap of plants to spread upon the ground."

And while the little boys were gone to get the grass, the mother, who was a sort of a witch, stood by the deer and made him come to life again. So just as the boys came back the deer got up and ran away.

The mother told them what she had done, but they did not answer her. They stood there in silence with their arms full of the bundles of grass. For a long time they did not say a word.

"What ails you?" asked the mother. "The people that come after us will do the same way. If they hunt a deer and do not kill him as they should, they must go after him again. Go, my sons, and follow him. Go both to-ether, the younger following the elder and watching the tracks."

So the brothers obeyed her, and flinging down the bundles of grass they ran after the deer.

(Song, sung by the mother.)

They went to the south, and many deer were there, but not the one they were seeking. They saw many tracks, but not the one they knew.

Song: Ha-ma-yo-whee-ee, etc.

They sang that now they would see the track, and then they would lose it again.

And they went on and on till they came to the Eastern Ocean.

Song: Ka-mé-to-ka-lá, etc.

At last they found the track they were after, and they saw the deer standing by the ocean.

Song: He-yo-ho
So-pa-ha, etc.

When the deer saw that he was pursued, he turned and ran on and on until he came to the Ocean of the West.

Song: A-kwa-kwe-ko, etc.

And when they came close behind him he jumped into the water, and they could not reach him to shoot him because he was in the water. And as the sun was setting and they could not kill the deer, they went home and lay down by the fire, one on either side, and when the mother spoke to them they would not answer her, for they were angry that she had made the deer to live.

"What ails you?" asked the mother. "Have you been fighting or did some accident happen to you? Look at the meal I am cooking for you and for no one else. Eat it and sleep, and in the morning I will show you how to hunt the deer. He is on a high mountain, and you must set fire to the mountain and he will run out and you can kill him."

So all night long the mother remained awake, sitting upon the housetop on a deerskin which she spread there; and she sang all night long, although there was a heavy fog and it began to rain.

Song: Ma-kai-ya-ma-kai, etc.

In the morning, when the sun rose, she went first of all to the mountain and set it on fire herself. When the two sons came she told the elder to go up on the mountain while the younger remained below; and while the elder searched upon the hilltop the younger shot the deer. The brothers killed it and sat beside it and talked of all they had done and suffered on their mother's account. They were so angry with her that they determined to skin the deer and cook and eat the meat without giving her a share.

And this they did,. and waited till sunset before they went down the mountain to their home. And among the rocks on the homeward journey they killed many rabbits, which they took home to their mother, but not a word did they tell her about their having killed and eaten the deer. This ends the story of the deer.

THE STORY OF THE EAGLES

THE boys were getting older now, and their hair was growing very long. It was down to their knees, but their mother told them she could not cut their hair because she was not a man. She told them, however, to get up very early the next morning and go to the place where there was an eagle's nest, and to bring the eagles home to her.

So they got up very early in the morning and went to the place where there was a nest of crows. "Perhaps this is what she means," they said; so they took the crows home with them and asked her if that was what she meant.

"No, that is wrong," said the mother, and she threw the crows away.

So then they went again till they came to the place where there was a horned owl's nest. "This must be the one," they said, and they took it home to their mother; but she said that was not the right one, and she threw it away.

And they started out again and found the common owl in its nest and took it home to their mother; but she said that was not the one, and threw it away.

Then they went again, and came to a nest of young buzzards, some of which were sitting on the tree. "We must be right now," they but the mother said that was not said, and took the buzzard home, an eagle, and she threw the buzzard away.

"Wait now till morning," said their mother. So they slept all night, and very early in the morning went on their way until they came to a stream of water, and on the other side was a high mountain.

They crossed the stream and climbed the mountain, and not far beyond sat down to rest.

Their mother had told them to wait in this spot to see what would happen.

Soon a white eagle came flying towards its nest with a deer in its claws. They watched it until they saw it fly into its nest. Then there came a black eagle with a big hare in its talons, and it flew in the same direction. So they followed its course until they came to the foot of a great rock, very steep and high, and on top of it was the eagle's nest, with two young ones in It. One was white and one was black and they flew about on top of the rock. But the boys could not catch them, for the rock was too steep to climb. (Song.)

"I wonder why mother sent us here on such an errand," said the boys. (Song.) They tried and tried to climb the rock, but it was too steep, and they fell back time after time, and all the while the eagles were growing older.

The boys began to cry and lament; and they stood and held their hands to the east, and got some white clay and with it they painted their cheeks. Then they held their hands to the west, and got some black clay. These were signs of sorrow and mourning. Tears ran down their cheeks. (Song.)

At last they determined that come what might they would climb the steep rock. "You go first," said the older. "No, it is you who must try it first." So they disputed for a time, till at last the younger started to climb the rock. On he went until with just one step forward he lost his balance and fell to the ground, where he was broken in pieces.

Song: A-ma-te-kis-ma, etc.

He lay at the foot of the rock with all his bones broken, but the older brother, who was a witch, sat down beside him and put all the bones together one by one. Then he spoke to him and told him to wake up. "Why, I have just been asleep," said the younger brother. "No, you were dead, but I made you alive again," said the older. "Now I will try to climb the rock myself. Turn your back and by no means look at me until I give you leave."

So the older brother stood and held up his hands to the sky and brought down a big red snake. The younger brother looked around and saw that the steep rock was full of red snakes, whose heads stuck out of every crevice, and the elder climbed among the snakes until he reached the top.

On top the rock was covered with snakes of all sorts, red snakes and gopher snakes and rattlesnakes, and the boy sat on the edge of the rock looking at the eagles' nest, but afraid to go near it for fear of the snakes.

Make haste and throw down the eagles," said the younger from the foot of the rock.

Song: Ha-mat-a-ku-ti-yai, etc.

The older sang a song to the snakes telling them he would not hurt them, but only wanted to catch the eagles. (Song.)

So he caught the eagles and tied their feet together.

Song: Ha-kán-a-mo-kán.

As he started down the rock he threw the eagles to the ground, and both of them flew directly to the feet of the younger, who caught them and refused to give them to his brother.

"Give me my eagles," said the older.

"No, I shall keep them for myself," said the younger. After a while, however, he agreed to give up the black eagle to his brother.

"And now you had better run home as fast as you can," said the older, "for if I am not mistaken it is going to rain." (Song.)

So the older brother held up his hands to the west and brought the rain. The clouds floated in and the sky was covered with them, and it began to rain in torrents just on the path where the younger brother was going. He tried to find shelter here and there, but the rain beat in everywhere. All this time the older brother went another road in the sunshine. He was very angry at his brother because he kept the white eagle from him.

Song: A-kwe-kwa
Ha-mat-a-whan, etc.
   (About a dozen lines.)

The younger brother suffered very much in the storm with the white eagle he was carrying. (Song.)

It rained so hard that at last the white eagle died. He was sitting on the ground beside the dead eagle when his brother went by looking at it.

The younger brother grew very angry. "You need not look so scornfully at me," he said. "You think I am young and cannot do anything, but you shall see that I can do things as well as you." So he stood and held up his hand to the north and called the thunderstorm to come (Song), and quick clouds came, and it rained very hard on the road the older brother took. The younger went another way where the sun shone bright and hot. He was hunting and killing rabbits as he went along. (Song.) "I told you what I was going to do," he said in his song.

The elder brother was suffering in the storm, from which he could find no shelter. He tried to shield the black eagle from the rain; but this he could not do, and the black eagle was already dying. (Song.)

At last the black eagle died and the brothers met again. "Why did you do this thing?" each asked the other. "I never heard of relatives treating each other so." So they shook hands and were friends again.

Then they made ready to bury the eagles. They dug a big hole, but the earth was black, and they said that that was not a fit place to bury the eagles. Gophers and rats would dig their bones and eat them. So they took them up and went to a place where the ground was yellow, and there they buried them. They made a great big hole and went down into it and buried the eagles there. Each brother cut off his own hair and dressed the eagles with it when they buried them.

Song: He-ko-ma-ta-ma, etc.

The sun was setting and it was growing late, so they went home and lay down one on either side of the fire.

The mother was cooking their supper, but when she brought it to them they would not eat.

"What ails you, my sons?" she said. "Here is the supper I cooked for you and for no one else, and in spite of all my pains you will not eat my food. Have you been fighting, and are you hurt?"

(Song.) The mother began to sing that the eagles were coming, but the oldest son woke from his sleep and told his mother she ought not to say what could not be true, for the eagles were dead. So he lay down again.

(Song.) But the mother sang and danced and saic that the eagles were coming. The boys made no answer, but laid there quietly.

Song: "I tell you, my sons, that the eagles are coming," repeated the mother.

"Get up and see if the eagles are coming," said the older to his brother. So the younger went out to look, and there was the white eagle coming, just as it was before it was buried. Then the elder brother got his eagle back too, and the mother scolded them for doing such things to each other. This ends the story of the eagles.

THE STORY OF THE CHAUP (CONTINUED)

THE mother of the boys told them that she was just like a man, since she knew everything. She had been all around the world and knew everything in it. And she com-manded them to bring her a certain tree, telling them where it grew, as she needed it for something she was going to do.

Next morning the brothers went as their mother had told them, and found the tree growing right in the middle of a pond; but the water about it was so deep and there were so many animals around the pond, that they were afraid to go into the water to cut it down.

Song: Ha-me-wá-me-e,
Hai-wa-ha-ha, etc.

Then the oldest son, who had a pipe stuck in his ears, took the pipe and smoked it, and blew the water back and frightened all the animals away, and dried up the water, so that they easily went and cut down the tree, chopped it up fine, and carried it home on their heads.

When they brought it to their mother she was very glad, and she chopped the wood up fine, and took the pieces and put them out in the sun to dry. And the pieces of wood as she touched them made sweet music.

Song: Kwa-la-há-le, etc.

Then the old woman decorated the pieces with the colored feathers of woodpeckers and the topknots of quails, and made them into flutes for her sons to play on.

Song: We-le-wha-cha-a-cha-a-cha.

So the brothers sat down facing the north, and played on the flutes such sweet music that the girls from the north came to them, attracted by the sound; but the boys did not like the girls from the north.

Song: We-le-wha-cha-a-tal, etc.

So they sat down facing the south, and played the same music so loud and so sweet that the girls from the south came to hear it, but they did not like them either, because they ate rats, snakes, and such animals as that, and their bodies did not smell good.

Song: Há-ma-kó-lu
Ha-ma-we-le, etc.

(Singer and Indian audience clapped hands in time.)

So they sat down toward the west, and played the beautiful music again, until the girls from the west came to them, but they did not like them, because they ate all the animals that live in the ocean.

Song: Há-ka-só-lu
Ha-ma-we
Ha-ma-ko-lu
Ha-ma-we-we-le-we
Ha-ma-cha.

But when they played the sweet music facing the east, some girls came from there, the daughters of Ith-chin, the buzzard, and they liked them because they lived on the fruit that grows in the east and they smelled sweet.

It was early in the morning when the girls first heard the music.

They were on their way to a pond where they used to swim every morning, and were looking for something they wanted to eat. It was the younger sister who first heard the music; and when she told her sister to listen to the wonderful sounds, the older could hear nothing. "Come stand where I am standing," said the younger, "and you will hear it plainly," but even then the older sister could not hear it.

"I must go, I must follow the music," said the younger, but her sister reproved her.

"If you mean to go to get married, this is no way to do to start empty-handed. A girl who is to be married takes presents to her mother-in-law and father-in law."

Their father, the turkey buzzard, knew what they were planning, and when they went home he asked what they had been doing by the pond.

The girls said they had been looking for the right kind of willow peel to weave into a dress.

So they went away one day towards where the boys lived, and from far away they looked back and saw their old home and sang a song of farewell.

Song: Kai-o-ñe

Ma-ha-qui-po-ke, etc.

And they travelled very far that day, until it grew so dark they could not see; so they sat down and took the pipes from their ears and smoked upon them and blew the night away. And it shone, there was light, and they found their way.

Song: Ma-ta-yan-he-peel-ya
Ma-ta-yan-ee-e-e-é-l-ya, etc.

Meaning, it was only the night they were afraid of, only the dark night.

And they went on through brush and thorns.

Song: Ma-ta-yan
Ta-li-cah
Ta-me, etc.

The brush and thorns are hurting us, they sang.

Ta-ya-wa-ha
E-ka-wa-ya-ka-me, etc.

There was no road, and they pushed their way through the brush suffering and crying on their way.

Song: Ha-ta-mo
Qua-ma-ya-whee, etc.

They came at last to a growth of willows high above their heads, and the younger sister grew so tired that she lagged far behind.

Song: Nau-ke-nau-me, etc.

"Come quickly," said the older sister. "I am too tired," she sang.

At last they came to a big sand mountain which they tried to climb, but every time they tried they slipped and fell back to the bottom again.

Song: Sa-llá-lle-a-llá-lle
Há-ke-pá-me, etc.

Meaning, they tried in vain to climb the mountain.

"What is the matter with you?" the younger sister asked the older.

"You say you are a witch, and yet you cannot contrive some way for us to climb the mountain." So the older sister stood and stretched up her hands and brought something from the sky like a fur mantle or hide and covered the mountain with it, so they climbed it easily and sat down on the top to rest.

In the distance they saw a pond of water, so they said they would rest a while and then go drink the water, and from there start on to the boys' home, which was not far away.

Half way to the pond they met a rattlesnake, whose back was very prettily painted. And they stood and watched him until he looked up and saw them.

"How did you happen to come over here, my nieces?" he asked.

"We heard some sweet music and came to follow it," they said.

"I am the one who played that music," said the snake. "Then play it again," they told him; and the rattlesnake tried his best to make music, but all he could do was to rattle his rattles.

Song: Ha-we-chu-me
Ha-ha-we-e-e-e, etc.

"You are too good a man to lie like that," they sang. "The best thing you can do is to keep quiet, or else you are likely to get hurt." (Indian auditors laugh.)

So they made mocking gestures and went on their way.

And they came to a house where the coon lived.

"What are you doing here?" said the coon; and the girls told him they were looking for the man who made the sweetest music they ever heard.

"I made the music," said the coon.

"Then make it again," they said; but all he could do was to run into his house and bring out a big gopher snake, which he promised to cook for supper if they would stay and eat it.

"We do not eat such things," they said, and they left him railing at them, and went on till they came to the horned owl's house, and he asked the same question, and at their answer told them that he was the one who made the music; but when they asked him to play it for them he could not do it, but promised them a snake for their supper if they would stay and share his meal.

They laughed at him and went on their way.

Song: Ho-sá-lu-la-ta-kwa, etc.

At last they came to the water which they had seen in the distance, and in the water was a tremendous frog that frightened them so they were afraid to drink; but they took the little baskets they wore on their heads and drove the frog away and drank the water.

Song: Mau-ha-ta-kum-ho-o-o-ma, etc.

They sang about the frog splashing in the water.

E-han-a-ta-ka-han-a, etc.

They sang to drive the frog away.

It was getting dark, and one of the plants they passed was making a curious noise. They stood and watched it and sang a song about it.

Song: Ha-mai-ko-te-e-hay-cha, etc.

The mother of the boys knew that the girls were coming, and she told her sons that when the girls came they must not allow themselves to care for them, or make any motion to greet them. If they were perfectly cold and silent to them, the girls would go away again to their home where they belonged.

That night the owls and coyotes howled and hooted around the house where the boys lived, and the mother said that something must be going to happen. It was an evil omen, for she never heard the owls and coyotes make such a noise before. She told the older son to go out towards the south and see what was going to happen; but he came back declaring that there was nothing to be seen.

But the coyotes and owls howled and hooted the more because the girls were coming, and the mother told her younger son to go out towards the north and see what was the matter.

He took his bows and arrows and went out of the house; but when he came back he said there was nothing anywhere about.

Just as he entered the house the girls came, and the mother was lying by the door inside the house. So the girls came and sat down in silence in front of the door where the mother could see them.

"Who are you?" asked the mother. "Are you my nieces--my sisters--my aunts--or any of my relations?"

To each of these questions the girls made no reply.

"Are you my daughters-in-law?" she asked at last; and to this question the girls replied very softly, "Yes."

"Then there are your husbands sleeping in the house. Go to them if you choose."

So the older and the younger sister went each to the bed of her husband and lay down beside him; but the elder son remembered his mother's command, and would not greet his wife; and when vexed at his silence she sent fleas and bugs to bite him, he would not move or stir.

Song (sung by the mother-in-law).

Song (sung by the sisters).

And in the morning the brothers rose very early and went out to saddle their horses, and the girls went out and sat outside. The mother-in-law told them that they could go to the pond to bathe, While they sat there the older sister said to the younger, "You are now a relative of the old woman since your husband loves you, but I am not, and I shall go back to my home."

"I shall be too lonely to stay without you," said her sister. "If you go I shall go with you."

So they went to the pond, bathed their faces and went home. The younger son was sick with grief for the loss of his wife. The older brother would go hunting and bring something home to his mother to eat, but she would give nothing to the younger son. "I told you not to care for the girl or to speak to her," she said. "Now you are pining away for her, and may die of your disobedience."

He pined and fasted for many days, until he was too weak to hunt anything but lizards and little animals on the hills, though he would tell his elder brother stories of the deer he pretended to have killed. At last his mother took pity on him when he was wasted nearly to death, and she threw him in the pond, and he grew well and fat again.

The younger brother used to beg the older to go away with him to seek their wives. His wife, he said, was going to have a baby, and lie must go to her; but the older brother, who cared nothing for his wife, would not at first agree to undertake the journey.

At last he yielded to his brother's wishes, and told his mother that he was going on a long journey. He took off a feather headdress that he wore and hung it up in the house. "Watch this every day that I am away," he said. "While I am living the feathers will remain as they are, but when I die they will move back and forth."

The younger son said farewell in the same way, and took a feather rope which he had made and stretched it across the house.

"Watch this carefully," he said, "for while I live it will remain as it is, but when I die it will be cut in two." And he promised that some day lie would come back to her again.

Song: Hay-a-ka-whin-ya, etc.

But the mother was sick with grief for the loss of her sons; she refused to let them go; and holding up her hands to the sky she brought down hailstones for them and told them to stay at home with her and play with the hailstones as they did when they were little. But already they were far away; and they looked back and said to her that when they were young she never brought hailstones down for them. Now they were old and must go away.

They went on till they came to a large grove of trees, and here they made stuffed figures of grass and put feathers around the head and waist of each, and stood them up and left them there. The old woman was in her bed, but looking out of the door she thought she saw her sons, and she ran to meet them and put her arms around them; but it was, only withered grass that she held in her arms. She fainted and fell to the ground. She did not know what to do.

Song: Ho-cha-ma-ta-we-wha, etc.

The boys went on looking for the track of the girls. They could only see a faint trace of their footsteps. The night came and they found a place to rest. The owls and coyotes howled very much. There was no road through the brush.

Song: Kwa-o-o-yo-o, etc.

All night the younger brother slept soundly, but the older could not sleep. He sat up and tied bunches of feathers on sticks which he stuck in a circle on the ground; and he sat down in the middle singing about the owls and coyotes that were hooting and howling around.

Song: Har-o-twa-me, etc.

At last he woke his brother and told him that he was afraid that something was going to happen, for the owls and the coyotes made such a noise.

"Why are you afraid?" asked his brother. "When the coyotes howl and the owls hoot it is a sign that they are beginning to get ready for the summer-time. There is no need to be afraid."

In the morning they travelled towards the girls' house, and they came to the same pool of water where the frog used to be. The older brother had gotten up first in the morning, and he said to the younger, "Make haste, it is getting late." So the older came first to the pond, and drank there and waited for his brother. Then the younger came to the water. "Take a drink of the water," said the older.

"No," answered his brother, "that is not a good place to drink. They used to kill people here."

"Lie flat on your stomach, and shut your eyes while you drink," said the older. He meant to drown his brother while his eyes were shut by pushing him into the water, and then go back to his home again.

Song: Whi-le-wi-ya-han
Whi-le-wi-ya-han, etc. [1]

The younger brother lay down to drink, but he did not shut his eyes. He was looking in the water, and just as he was getting ready to drink he saw in the water the reflection of h s brother, who bent over to push him in; and jumping up quickly asked if he was meaning to drown him.

"I was only killing a fly upon your neck," said his brother.

"I know well enough you want to kill me," said the younger, and he got up without drinking the water.

From there they travelled till they came to the top of a high mountain, and the elder came first to the top and sat down, and then the younger came, and they watched the people in the valley where a large crowd was playing a game of ball.

"Look at all those people," said the older. "How are we going to be able to get to the place in safety?"

So the younger stood up and held up to his hands to the sky, and got a lot of stars and put them all over his body. And his brother did the same, and they sat down and were watching the people. They were shining like stars.

____

[1] Up to this point I have used English pronunciation for songs. After this, a modified Spanish; English not being sufficiently phonetic.

Song: Ha-mai-nau-e-chak-om-whi-i-i, etc.

They rose as if they had wings, and flew over to where they wanted to go.

Song: Ha-che-nau-e-cha-kom-whi-i-i, etc.

I am going to fly to the girls' house," said the younger. "Watch me very closely and you will see where I go in among the crowds of people."

"We will die for the sake of the girls," said the older. "And we shall never see our home again."

The older watched his brother and saw him fly towards the houses in the midst of all the people. Among all the houses he did not know where to go; but he came to one of the houses where there was a crowd of people about it, and the roof opened and lie went in shining like a star. As he flew over their heads the people looked up and saw the Chaup. They wanted to catch him, but they could not. The father of the girls was there, and he told the people not to catch him, as that was not a star but a person. When the roof opened he went into the house, and here he found his wife.

Song: Ha-che-nau-e-cha-kom-whi-i-i, etc.

The older brother, left alone on the mountain, flew after his brother shining like Chaup. People tried to catch him in the same way, but the girls' father warned them again, and he too went into the house, where he found his wife.

The girls were glad to see their husbands, and laughed so loud that their father heard them from outside and said: "I wonder what is the matter with my daughters. They never make a noise like that. Go and see what is the matter with them," he said to his grandson; and he gave him a shell full of wheat to eat on the way. The little boy went along eating and playing till he finished all the wheat, and then he came back without any news. So the old man gave him a shell full of corn, and the little boy went along eating the corn till he came to the house, and peeped inside and saw the brothers there with eyes shining like fire; and he was afraid of them, they shone so bright and clear. So he ran back as fast as he could.

"What is the matter?" asked the grandfather.

"There is something like stars in the house. They have eyes of fire, and I was afraid."

When the old man heard this he wanted to kill the Chaups; so he went to the house of the coyote and asked him if he was willing to kill them for him. The coyote took up his bow and arrow and went to the house; but when he saw the brothers they were shining so bright he could not go near them. So he went back and told the old man that nothing could hurt them. They were great wizards with eyes of fire that made him afraid.

So the old man could not find any one to kill them until he went to a place where there were a great many hawks, and he asked if they were willing to kill the Chaups. They agreed and said that they would tear them in pieces with their beaks.

Song: Mi-kan-ám-a-ha, etc.

So the hawks flew to the house where the Chaups were and tried to kill them; but they were afraid, and they met the old man on the way home and told him they could not do anything.

So then he went to the bear's house, and asked him if he would kill them. He consented and said that he would scratch them and tear them in pieces with his claws.

The bear went to the house and scratched around the door, but did not dare to touch the Chaups, and told the old man he'd better find some one else to do it for him. So the old man went home determined to do it himself, since no one else would dare to. So he dug a passage underground from his house towards the girls' house, and when he dug under the house it began to fall with a loud noise; and the brothers flew out among the people, who followed them saying they were Chaups and trying to kill them; but since they were witches no one could hurt them.

So they all returned home and met the old man going out alone with his bow and arrow. "Where are you going?" they asked him. "You are too old to do anything by yourself."

"I am going to look at them," he said; and he went on till he caught up with the Chaups. He was a wizard too; and as he came up to the younger brother he killed him first. Then the younger called out to the older to save himself; but when the older looked back and saw his brother dead, he said he might as well die too. He would be so lonely. So he sat down on the ground, and the old man came and killed him too.

And he called out very loud to the people to come and see his dead enemies. "I think I hear some one calling," said the coyote; and when he saw the Chaups were dead he called to the people and said it was he who had killed them. And all the people left their houses and gathered together and told the two sisters to sing about the dead Chaups, and they sang that they had killed them under the trees.

Song: To-mé-to-mí, etc.

But the old man pushed them aside and sang by himself.

Song: A-llan-a-hi, etc.

He stood on the breast of the dead Chaups and sang that it was he who had killed them.

Song: Ha-whai-cha-hi-i-i-i, etc.

Then he told the people to cut them in pieces and eat them. And the people gathered together and cut them up and ate them.

The wife of the dead Chaup knew that as soon as her baby was born, if it was a son the old man would kill it and eat its brains.

He had a little olla ready to put the brains in; but when the child was born the mother pretended that it was a girl; and the old man was so angry that he took the olla and threw it at the mother and broke it on her head.

The baby boy grew so fast that while the people were still eating his father's body he cried for a piece, which they would not give him. He did not know it was his father.

His grandmother, the mother of his mother, told him that that was his father's body they were eating.

When the boy grew older the old grandfather tried many ways to kill him, but could not because the boy was a witch. The grandfather once dug a big hole in the ground and filled it full of water and set up sharp stakes in it under the water and told the little boy that he had made it for him to swim and dive in. The boy knew that he wished to kill him, but he swam about in it and nothing hurt him.

Another time the grandfather took a big rock and told the boy to play with it by throwing it up in the air, expecting that it would fall upon him and kill him; but the boy knew his purpose, and he threw the rock up in the air but got out of its way when it came down.

His grandmother used to take the bones of his father and put feathers with them and put them upon her body and go out and dance by herself. The little boy used to see her dance, and one day the thought came to him that these were the bones of his father. He had an uncle who loved him very much, and he asked this uncle for a bow and arrow; and when his uncle gave it to him, he went to the place where his grandmother used to dance, and he asked his uncle to dig him a hole in the ground, as he wanted to play in it. The uncle did this to please him, and just as the sun was setting the boy went into the hole and hid there.

The old woman came as usual to the place to sing and dance; and the little boy shot and killed her. When the people came running to the dead woman, he said it was he who had killed his grandmother. When they tried to seize him he went into the ground, and they could not find him. He came out again in another place, but they could not hurt him because he was a witch.

One day he saw the bone of his father's heel made into a painted ball, and the people played with it for a shinny-ball. The boy knew it was his father's bone, and so he stood far away and whistled and sang, and the ball rolled to his feet and he took it up and threw it far out into the ocean. When he threw that ball away they brought out another ball of the same kind; and he knew it was his uncle's bone, that of the older Chaup, and he was very sorry. And he stood towards the east and the ball came rolling to his feet, and with his feet he threw it far away to the east. Then he was glad and sang and danced.

Song: Cuy-a-ho-marr, etc.

He sang that he was the Chaup because he was the son of Chaup. His mother called him by this name, Cuy-a-ho-marr.

He used to sleep with his grandfather, and one time his grandfather told him that the chief must lead the people, and they must be willing to obey him. So he told him to get up on the housetop and proclaim that Cuy-a-ho-marr was to lead them, and command them to bring their bows; and if the people called out and accepted him he could live, but if they kept silent he must die. The boy agreed, and in the morning the new chief got upon the housetop, and all the people agreed to his words, so he knew he was to live and not die.

One day all the people went to another place to play peon [1] with the people there, and they got beaten. The grandfather went, and the little boy went afterwards and told his grandfather that he was going to play the game, and he would beat all the people of the other pueblo. But his grandfather forbade him to play with the strangers, saying that he would be killed by them. But the boy played and won, and burned all their houses and fields.

In the morning after he had beaten the game they all went home. As they were going along, the old man had a little basket full of wheat, but the little boy's basket was empty. He asked his grandfather for some of his wheat, but the grandfather would

---

[1] A famous gambling game.

not give him any. The boy said he was going to grind. So he did, and ate.

As they went on the way, the people who had killed his father were ahead with his grandfather. He was behind and got lost. His uncle was looking for his nephew, fearing that some one might have killed him. He was with them, but they could not see him. When they saw him his uncle called out to him, and they asked him to lead the way. So he went ahead and came first to a big rock. He made a path through the rock, and then climbed on top of it. The people went through the rock, and as they went in one by one the rock shut tip and killed all the people that had killed his father. He jumped down to see if any were left alive, but there was not one.

Song: Po-co-bo-kim, etc.

When the little boy came to his house he told all the people who had remained at home that those who were coming back were thirsty and wanted water. He told them to get water and go to meet them.

And all the people, young and old, that were at home went with water to look for the others and all died on the way. He had killed every one from that place except his grandfather, his aunt, his uncle, and mother. These were the only ones left.

And now he thinks of going to his old grandmother, the one left away off, the mother of his father. His mother and aunt used to make him sleep with them so they could watch him; but for three days he got up very early every morning; and, when they missed him, he said he was hunting. But his grandfather knew what he was planning to do. One day he went away and never came back. When the boy had gone his grandfather looked for him and went in all the houses of the others, and asked if they could not find him. The coyote hunted for him for four days, each day in a different direction, till at last he found tracks that went towards the east. He came home and told them that he had found tracks going to the east where the old grandmother lived; and they all went after him, following the tracks of the boy.

At last they found marks upon the ground which showed that he had been playing there, and then they knew that they were on the right road,

Song: E-ña-me-wha, etc.

Those that followed were singing this. His aunt, uncle, and mother started together, and his uncle caught up with him first, tired and worn out, and asked his nephew why he had run away from his home. He said he was going away and would never come back again, and he advised his uncle to go back to his house.

Song: E-wan-i-chau-ah-wa, etc.

Then his aunt caught up with him and asked him the same question, and he made her the same answer that he was never going back.

Song: In-i-si-in-i-si
Han-a-mak-a-ha, etc.

Then he went on again towards the home of his grandmother.

On the way he came to a big cañon where they had killed his father and uncle, and an owl went hooting before him. He tried to shoot it but could not hit it, and it kept on flying in front of him till it led him to the spot. Red ants, flies, and all sorts of insects were thick there. The ants had made paths where they went back and forth.

Song: Ah-yó-na-ki-yó-na-ki, etc.

He was standing there when his father's voice spoke to him, and told him that his bones were all broken in pieces and he could not do anything; so the boy sat down and tried to fit the bones into their places. He put all too-ether but the leg; and that he could not join so it would stand up. He could not do anything with it.

Song: Na-wa-mi-he-cha-whai-o, etc.

He was sorry and cried and went away.

Song: Nau-wa-ri-nau-i-i, etc.

After he left that place he came to a house where there were lots of lions. He stood at a distance and was thinking how he could get by. So he made himself into an old man, thinking that perhaps they would not kill him in that shape; but not being sure of that, he made himself into a young man, and then into a little boy; and he took fire and burned his head and made sores on his head, and went to the lions' house, where he found no one but a little boy of his own size. The little boy said nothing to him, but went and told the lions that his cousin had come to see him. He was still there when the lions came back. They brought rabbits and other kinds of game and began cooking them, but gave nothing to the little boy, who was picking up little bits of meat. There was a red-hot olla on the fire, and they put it on his head when he did not know it. He fainted and fell back. He was sick, and when he got up he asked the old man to doctor him.

The old man said all the people must come together in one house and he would doctor him there.

So all the people got together in one house.

Song: Kwi-nau-wi, etc.

After they doctored him he left the house, and there was a big stone before the house, and he shut the door with it and got on top of the house. The house fell and killed all the people.

From there he came to a pond where there were lots of blackbirds by the water, and he was afraid of them; and as he came nearer he heard the birds say, "Who is that? Kill him."

When he heard them say that, he threw a big stick and hit them on the legs and killed some, and the others flew away.

And he went on and came to a wide lake, and just as he came to the other side of it he turned back and saw his mother following him, and she was tired; and he took his bow and it spread out long, and he told her to walk on it across the lake. Just as she came near to him he took the bow away, and she fell into the water and was drowned. He had killed his mother.

He went on till he came to a big water, and he saw a big crane standing in the water, and the crane took hold of him and swallowed him by the feet; and just as his head was going down he called to a buzzard for help; and the buzzard flew down and took hold of him and dragged him out.

He came to a hill and stood on the hill and saw his grandmother, who was sitting there and looking towards him. He came to her, but she could not see him. She was blind. He sat on her lap, and she put her arms around him, and they both cried. When he came to the house it was full of heaps of dirt, and he cleaned it and burned the house down. "Where shall we go now?" asked his grand-mother. "I have no house." "Where do you want to go?" he asked. "I will take you wherever you choose." "I will go anywhere with you," she said. So he sat down and she climbed upon his back, and he flew with her far away to the north to the San Bernardino Mountains, and Chaup lives there now with his grandmother.

Constance Goddard Du Bois.

WATERBURY, CONN.

CEREMONIES AND TRADITIONS OF THE DIEGUENO INDIANS

INTRODUCTION[1]

THE following pages, discussing mainly the relations existing between the religious practices and religious beliefs--the ceremonies and the traditions--of the Diegueño Indians of Southern California, may be regarded as supplementary to a parallel but fuller treatment of the neighboring Luiseños. [2] The Diegueños are of Yuman stock, the Luiseños Shoshonean; but the two tribes are very similar in general culture, and, as has been pointed out, one has evidently greatly influenced the religious life of the other.

---

[1] Contributed as part of the Proceedings of the California Branch of the American Folk-Lore Society.
[2] "The Religion of the Luiseño Indians of Southern California" (Univ. Cal. Publ. in Amer. Arch. Ethn. [in press]).

A DANCE-SONG FROM MANZANITA

THIS includes Tutomunp, a Mohave dance-song, and Kachawharr, a Jacumba dance-song, accompanied by a basket rubbed with a stick. Hatakek of Manzanita is to sing the Diegueño song Kachawharr with basket accompaniment; but he begins by singing part of Tutomunp, a dance which originated with the Mohave Indians. The song always begins at sunset; and all these Western Indian songs have a "starter," the interpreter explains. The "starter" in this case is in the Mohave language, so the Diegueño interpre-ter attempts no translation.

The old man chants on and on, showing the most wonderful lungpower, continuing for five or ten minutes at a time, and ending each song or section of the song with a loud "Hup!"

Again he begins, and continues his loud and monotonous singing, for another five minutes or so. The tone of the chant varies. It rises to a higher pitch, "Hup!"

The same song again; and by this time a circle of men and women should be dancing, so the old man keeps time with his foot to show the measure of the dance. "Hup!"

For the next half-dozen songs he gives the translation in Diegueño. They relate to two brothers whose father is Homati-milya. [1] The names are all in the Mohave language. [1]

---

[1] Evidently the Mohave Matevilye.

Another song with varied tones ending in "Hup!" The meaning of the song: "They are going along. All is dim and hazy before them."

Song: More excited, with varied cadences. The singer keeps time with his foot. The song ends suddenly, "Hup!"

Song: Monotonous beginning, varied tones at end. Meaning: "We are going on. We have a long way to go."

Song: "We are going on. Many people live in other places, but we go on alone."

Another song: "We are going on, but some day we may meet somebody coming."

Now begins the dance-song of the Diegueños themselves, Kachawharr. This was taught the Manzanita people by those of Jacumba. All these dances are of course religious ceremonies. The singer, or leader of the dance, old Hatakek, takes a flat bowl-shaped basket turned upside down, and, part of the time seated, but mostly kneeling on the ground, he alternately rubs and taps this as if it were a drum, keeping time to the music of his chant.

Song: This is about the two brothers, the gods Tuchaipa and Yokomatis or Yokomat (the two names are sometimes given in one: Chaipakomat), who came forth from the ground at Jacumba, at the hot-spring there. Meaning of the song: "They

---

[1] One of these songs was obtained on a phonograph record (American Museum of Natural History, no. 1017), described in the paper now in press at the University of California.

are at Jacumba. They do not know where they came from. They came forth from the earth."

Song: "Let us build a house. It is going to rain." A hill at Jacumba is the house they built covered with earth. There is a hot-spring at the south of the hill, and this is the door of the house. [1]

Song: They were in the house at night and it began to rain on them.

Song: It leaked on them through the holes in the brush covered with sand. One brother was tapping on the roof of the house with a club (as the curving basket is tapped with the stick).

Song: He tells the other it is all right. "We have made it good and solid." He came out of the house and felt on the ground with his hands. The tobacco-plant was growing there. He could not see it in the darkness, but he could feel it. "It is ready to bloom."

Song: It was bigger the next time he felt it. He felt all around.

All kinds of plants are beginning to grow. The rain has started them in the night." He felt the plants. They were shaking in the wind.

Song: The brothers are talking of how they can gather seeds when the plants are ripe. The plants are growing fast in the rain, but they have no wives to gather the seeds.

---

[1] The primitive houses of the Luiseños and Diegueños were made of uprights and rafters of solid timbers, joined by wattled brush, the whole covered with earth, with an opening in front for a door, and a hole in the roof to permit the egress of smoke and the entrance of light, the house looking at a distance like a hillock of sand.

Song: When the wind blows, the plants look like the waves of the sea. It is a fine sight.

The old singer, squatting on bended knees, pounds gently on the basket which rests on his lap. Then he rubs it with the stick. Chawharr is said to mean "rubbing." He holds the stick with his right hand, the basket with the other. He rises by straightening his body, pounds more loudly, and sings louder. He moves his body up and down in time to the song. Song and movements stop suddenly, as is always the case in these dances. The old man is exhausted. This is hard work, and he is unaccustomed to it, since these dances are no longer performed, and it is many years since he has led the song.

He begins again, hitting the basket gently in time, and rubbing it at intervals.

The song is short, ending suddenly. It means: "They are going to make smoke out of the tobacco-plant. It is ready now to bring into the house."

Now they are going towards the west after the girls whom they wish for their wives. They run with balls, kicking the ball with their foot, running after it, throwing it again with the foot. With three bounds of the ball they reach the ocean where the girls are. But they do not stay. They turn and go back home, their hair flying in the wind, the east wind. [1]

____

[1] This and the following songs recall similar incidents in the Cuyaho-marr story, which would seem to be merged with the history of the two gods; or by some omitted connection, the two stories may both be celebrated in this dance. As the full recital lasts all night, it was impossible for Hatakek to give more than a portion of it.

Song: The girls get to thinking why the boys came.

Song: The brothers come home and see their plants ripe. "Who will gather the seeds? We need women for the work."

Song: They hunt cotton-tail rabbits at Jacumba.

Song: They are trying to see who can shoot the farthest. They begin to gamble with bow and arrows according to the length of their shots. The younger brother loses all the time. He comes home with nothing.

Song: They try another game. They first shoot one arrow. Then whoever comes close to the first arrow wins. The younger loses again.

Song: They gamble again, springing sticks edgewise. The younger gets thin. The elder wins everything.

Song: The younger begins to stake and to lose his fingers, arms, legs, all the parts of his body. He begins to wager every hair of his head. Nothing is left but his heart. "We will play with these long poles with hoops. I will stake my heart. If you win, you can eat it."

Song: They go east and get long poles and begin to straighten them in the fire to play with. The younger loses his heart and falls down dead. The elder sees him dead and dances all around him.

Song, with basket accompaniment. The old man rises on his knees and pounds vigorously. Meaning: "He began to skin and eat him."

Song, with basket accompaniment as before: The Coyote brings a big load of wood and drops it on the ground. The brother tells Coyote he will roast (burn?) the body.

Song, with basket: The elder brother is behind the house. He sees a little bird flying there. He thinks it is the spirit of his dead brother.

Song, slow time, with basket, more excited than ever at the end. Meaning: He sees many birds fly out. He is afraid and wants to run away. He goes south through piles of rocks where the trail leads. He gets hungry and pulls up fresh yucca-plants to cook and eat. He looks at the plants.

Song: He sees deer-tracks going toward the water.

Song: He goes on towards the desert, and sees a band of mountain-sheep, which he frightens, and they run away from him. He is talking to them.

Last song: He goes to the Maricopa Indians. [1]

---

[1] It is said that in this dance the singers alternate, one man taking up the song when the other stops.

AWIKUNCHI, A FAIR-WEATHER-MAKING CEREMONY

THERE all is fragmentary, the connections between external objects and the ideas they stand for must become obliterated by time; and if the story is given at second-hand, little can be learned with precision. Most of the writer's material has been gathered directly from the old men who are the only real authorities; but Sant, the Diegueño interpreter, told the little that he remembers to have heard about the Awikunchi ceremony.'

Awikunchi is the name of a certain rock in the middle of which there had been carved the figure of a tiny coiled snake. When a man makes a hole in this rock, it will grow together again. It is the only rock that is known to have this property.

Finding that it was within accessible distance, I went to see it. It is a large, low, sloping rock of soft, loose granite; but it was with difficulty that the carved figure of the snake could be seen, for this had been damaged by some iconoclast who had dug it partly away, perhaps in the expectation of seeing it grow again.

In the old days no one could be found so sacrilegious as to deface such an object; but American influence is shown in the younger generation, who have been robbed of their past and preserve no reverence for it.

The connection between the rock and the song-series which bears its name could not be discovered. This series was sung for fair weather. If it rains for some time, they may say, "Let us sing

Awikunchi to end the rain." So they sing all night to the accompaniment of a basket rubbed by a stick; and perhaps the rain stops in the morning.

The story of the songs is forgotten; but Sant recalls a mere fragment. A certain number refer to a boy named Kwilyu, who could eat more than any one in the world. His father grew tired of a son who ate so much, and planned to run away and leave him. So he made himself a boat. And he went out in it to the islands of the ocean. He thought the boy could not catch him there; but he could not escape in this way, for Kwilyu overtook him. The forgotten sequel of the story may never be known.

BELIEFS

CINON Duro (Hokoyel Mutawir), the last hereditary chief at Mesa Grande, a living repository of the knowledge of the past, felt more keenly than any of the old men the lasting value of the ancient rule of life. It was sacrilege to reveal the religious mysteries to a stranger, or even to hint at the sacred ritual so solemnly imposed. His affection for the writer and his consciousness that the past was to die with him, led him to give for friendship what could never have been bought for money. But the struggle between his inbred reluctance to reveal the things of the past, and his promise to do so, led him to give the recital in the briefest way.

A satisfactory rendering of this recital could be given only by an interpreter combining a full knowledge of old Indian terms with a good acquaintance with the English language; and such a one was not often to be found at Mesa Grande, where most of the younger Indians know only enough of their mother tongue for conversation with parents and grandparents in the house. Any Diegueño word not in common use, any allusion to the myths, the gods, or ceremonies, is foreign to them. [1] It is extremely fortunate that in the Manzanita region an excellent interpreter was found, familiar with the rare terminology of the past. The loss is great that in the death of Cinon Duro, September 17, 1906, there must die many a secret of the past.

---

[1] The Mesa Grande Chaup story (Journal of American Folk-Lore, 1904, vol. xvii, pp. 217-241) is an exception, being well interpreted.

The ceremonies which Cinon performed and the ancient religion he adhered to had been carefully taught to him by his father, that they might be transmitted to posterity with exact detail. The myths and sacred songs had been acquired in the same way. His father's name was mentioned with the greatest reverence in a half-whisper, since the names of the dead are spoken with reluctance. Where his father gained this knowledge was not distinctly explained, though it was stated that all religious ritual had been devised and directly given by Tuchaipa himself.

It is extremely interesting to trace the reciprocal influence of the two tribes, Luiseño and Diegueño, each upon the other as shown in the surviving fragments of their ancient worship. To one who has long studied the subject it becomes increasingly evident that many of the ceremonials used among the Diegueños were acquired directly from their neighbors the Luiseños, as the latter declare. The toloache initiation ceremony, the eagle fiesta, and the whirling eagle-feather dance are the ones especially stated to have been thus introduced.

The value of the Chungichnish worship as a conquering faith has been noted. The Luiseños declare that they received it themselves from their brethren of the coast. It is not probable that it displaced an earlier and more primitive religion, but much more likely that its ritual became fused and blended with whatever of the sort already existed in both tribes. It would be impossible at this late day to disentangle all these associations and to make positive assertions in regard to the matter, but the statement made by the Luiseños that some of the sacred songs sung by the Diegueños in their ceremonies are in the Luiseño language may be possible of verification later. Certain it is that the language of these songs is acknowledged by the Diegueños to be foreign or unknown to themselves.

The differences between these two tribes are very striking, and based on deep-lying racial factors. The Dieguenos' natural affiliations are with the Mohaves, Maricopas, Havasupais, etc. The great creator-gods Tuchaipa and Yokomatis are held in reverence. Diegueno mythology deals with characters powerful in themselves, and representative of those who are to come after; as, for example, Sinyohauch, the wonder-working woman, typical of the various powers of Nature; and Cuyahomarr, the wonder-working boy, who gives names to all the plants and animals in the world. These characters have no counterparts in Luiseno mythology, which is subtler, less dramatic, and more metaphysical than the Diegueno. The death of Tuchaipa has many of its details either lent to the Luisenos or borrowed from their moon myth, the sickness and death of Moyla the Moon in its waning, and its rebirth as the crescent in the resurrected Ouiot.

All tribes with early affiliations with Mexico might naturally adopt the myth of a dying god or demi-god, but these influences are lost in obscurity. It will be found an important and perhaps not a hopeless task to trace the reciprocal give-and-take in two tribes so racially distinct and geographically and socially conjoined as the so-called Luisenos and Dieguenos.

On review of the notes of Cinon's conversations, it appears that in his account of the toloache ceremony he mentions Wanawut, not by that Luiseno term of course, but by saying that "the boys jumped in a ditch which had a redo (woven net), with stones in it, in the bottom of it."

In describing the girls' ceremony, he remarked that red, white, and black were the colors for women.

Such of the Luiseño form of ritual as was adopted by the Diegueños of Mesa Grande seems to have been introduced about a hundred and twenty years ago. In the two tribes there were some minor differences in performance. Instead of the lump of sage-seed and salt, rabbit-meat and salt were put into the girl's mouth in the ceremony Wukunish. Instead of the dry root of the toloache, a freshly-dug piece was pounded and the juice expressed in the boys' initiation ceremony.

In the Story of Creation as he first gave it, Cinon did not mention any primeval existence antedating Earth and Sky; but on a later occasion he sang the songs referring to the birth of the creator-gods, and mentioned in an obscure way the First Existence, typified in Luiseño myths by Kivish Atakvish. If he had lived, the Diegueño version of this most obscure and important part of the Creation myth would probably have been heard, since a few hours before the accident which resulted in his death he promised next time to tell "a part of the Creation story he had never yet related."

The words of the Songs of Creation which he sang, and which were recorded on the graphophone, are as follows:--

First song, sung by the Sky father who begot the creator-gods Tuchaipa and Yokomatis:--

Yi-haw-ma-ya-a i
Yi-haw-ma-ya-a i (repeated six times)
(A long sigh repeated)
Ich-a-pa-wha-chi-ho
Yo-o-o
Ich-a-pa-wha-chi-yo
Yo-o-o
Ma-to Tu-chai-pa
Mai-i-i Yo-ko-mat

Ich-a-pa-wha-chi-yo
Icha-a-pa-wha-chi-yo.

The second song by the Earth mother describes the bringing forth of the creator-gods:--

Chu-pa-chu-wha
Wi-i-i
Chu-pa-chu-wha
Wi-i-i
Tu-chai-pa
Chu-pa-chu-wha
I-i-i
Yo-ko-mat-is
Chu-pa-chu-wha
Wa
Wi-i-i
Wi-i-i.

The weird intonation of the chant, and its strange changes, cannot be described, nor the intense reverence for the old religion expressed in every look and gesture.

SIGNIFICANCE OF MYTHS

THE Luiseño story of the dying Ouiot who became the moon, and the Diegueño story of the dying creator-god Tuchaipa, probably originated in some source common to both tribes; but while the Luiseños derive all their ceremo-nials from the deliberations of the first people in council assembled, related with an almost historical precision, the Diegueños find the sanction for each of their religious customs in some event in a myth. The first Image ceremony was performed to celebrate the death of Tuchaipa, when the people were still at Wikami; [1] but, no one knowing how to perform it, they sent to a mysterious being, Maiheowit, who lived in the islands of the ocean, to ask him for instruction. [2]

The reason for the Diegueño Image dance in the ceremony for the dead is to be found in the Cuyahomarr myth. Sinyohauch, having killed her son by cruelty, was forced to dance carrying his decayed body in her hands. The following is a realistic description of this: "The long hair had partly fallen out, but what was left upon the scalp, lifted by the wind, waved up and down as she danced and sang, carrying the body. She sang the song of the Image dance. This was the first time any one made a dance for the dead. These were the First People; and as they did, all must do who come after. This is the reason they have the Wukaruk ceremony."

---

[1] Mohave Avikwame, Dead Mountain, in southern Nevada.
[2] Compare the Mohave myth summarized in Journal of American Folk-Lore, 1906, vol. xix, p. 315. See, also, American Anthropologist, 1905, vol. vii, p. 627.

Further sanction for the Image dance in this ceremony is found in the same myth, as follows: "He came to the spot where his father and uncle had been killed; and, coming first to his uncle's grave, he put his hand in the ground, and reached down and pulled him out. He set him there before him; but his uncle said, 'You can do nothing for me. My bones are all dust, and are mixed with seeds in the earth.' So he put him back, and went to his father's grave and pulled him out in the same way. But it was the same as before. 'You can do nothing for me,' said his father. 'But what you have done, the people that come after will do. They will bring back their dead to look at them once more' (in the Image dance)."

Cuyahomarr also originated the custom of cutting the hair in mourning for the dead, still practised by many. "The boy's hair had grown long; and he set fire to a bunch of tall grass that grows on the desert, and, putting his head in the fire, he began to burn his hair off. Then, seeing in his shadow that one side of his hair was still long, he put his head again in the fire and burned it off even all around. This is why they still cut the hair for the dead and bum it in the fire."

I have found no other myth-tale in either tribe in any way similar to the Cuyahomarr story. It has unity, consistency, and what we should call a dramatic sense which makes it still impressive as fiction. Even among the younger Indians the memory of it lingers in a fragmentary way. Sinyohauch remains a type of extraordinary power in woman. Some of the older Indians who are Catholics have identified her with the Virgin Mary.

The Luiseño creation myth [1] shows less of the inventive instinct of the story-teller, and more of the power of abstract thought and intellectual conception. This remarkable survival from the past must serve to rank the Luiseños high in the ethnic scale.

---

[1] Journal of American Folk-Lore, 1904, vol. xvii, p. 185.

YUMA CREATION MYTH, AS TOLD BY A DIEGUEÑO

AN old Yuma told the Diegueño interpreter Sant how the gods Tuchaipa and Yokomat [1] first came into being.

When they came forth from the Earth mother, they had to pass through the ocean, which then covered the land; and the first-born, Tuchaipa, came up through the water with his eyes shut, so that he got through all right; but when his brother called to him to ask him how he managed it, he told him that he came through with his eyes open.

So Yokomat came with wide-open eyes through the ocean, and the salt water hurt his eyes and made him blind.

Each brother had brought an animal with him. Tuchaipa had the badger, and Yokomat the swift. The badger was rough and furry, and the swift's feathers were smooth and fine.

After they came out, when his brother could not see, Tuchaipa changed the animals, taking the swift for himself.

"What have you done?" asked his brother. "This is not my animal. This one is rough and furry."

"Yes, that is yours," said Tuchaipa.

---

[1] Or Yokomatis. Tuchaipa and Yokomat are the Diegueño creator-gods.

But Yokomat was so angry that he went down into the ground again.

So Tuchaipa made the world by himself.

He made all the people. First he made the men, and then the women. The women were very hard to make.

Then he made the moon to give them light; but, finding that the moon was not bright enough, he made the sun to light the world.

WATERBURY, CONN.

www.ingramcontent.com/pod-product-compliance
Lightning Source LLC
Chambersburg PA
CBHW061108100726
47911CB00012B/464